Fairy Godmother's Palace

Fairy Godmother

Miss Flutterbee

To the memory of my mother, D. K. Holabird,
a magical spirit —K. H.

To Holly and Olivia, who liked pink —S. W.

LITTLE SIMON

An imprint of Simon & Schuster Children's Publishing Division
1230 Avenue of the Americas, New York, New York 10020
First Little Simon hardcover edition February 2020
Text copyright © 2014 by Katharine Holabird
Illustrations copyright © 2014 by Sarah Warburton
Originally published in Great Britain in 2014 by Hodder Children's Books
All rights reserved, including the right of reproduction in whole or in part in any form.
LITTLE SIMON is a registered trademark of Simon & Schuster, Inc.,
and associated colophon is a trademark of Simon & Schuster, Inc.
For information about special discounts for bulk purchases, please contact
Simon & Schuster Special Sales at 1-856-506-1949 for business@simonandschuster.com.
Manufactured in China 1119 SCP
2 4 6 8 10 9 7 5 3 1
Cataloging-in-Publication Data is available from the Library of Congress.
ISBN 978-1-5344-2917-8
ISBN 978-1-5344-2918-5 (eBook)

Twinkle
Thinks Pink!

Katharine Holabird and Sarah Warburton

LITTLE SIMON

New York London Sydney Toronto New Delhi

Twinkle bounced out of bed, gave her wings a shake,
tapped her toes, and skipped downstairs to her friends,
leaving a trail of fairy dust behind her.

"Tra-la-la-la-la!" she sang.
"I'm a little fairy,
and I love things that are PINK~
like pink balloons, pink lollipops,
and strawberry fizzy drinks!"

"Tomorrow is Fairy Godmother's garden party,"
Twinkle announced, picking up the invitation on the doormat.
"Everyone says the royal roses look pretty as a picture."

"I'll eat lots of
fairy cakes!"
shouted Pippa.

"I'll wear my
sparkly outfit,"
said Lulu.

Dear Twinkle,
Make my wishes
come true and
come to my party
From: Fairy Godmother

RSVP

"And I'll do cartwheels for Fairy Godmother," said Twinkle, who loved to dance.

The three little fairies zoomed off through Sparkle Tree Forest.
Twinkle fluttered her wings, flying loop-the-loops and chasing Lulu
and Pippa at top speed. Before long, the fairies were high up in the sky.

"Ooooh!" cried Twinkle, pointing below.
"There's the palace garden! Let's take a look. . . ."

The fairies admired all the beautifully colored roses, spread out like a rainbow for the party.

"What a shame there aren't more pink ones," said Pippa.
"Easy peasy!" said Twinkle. "I can change them any way you want."
She'd seen Fairy Godmother wave her wand and make color
wishes; surely it couldn't be that hard?

Twinkle closed her eyes,

waved her wand in circles,

twirled around,

and cast a little spell.

"Roses are red,
that's what I think,
but now let's make
all roses PINK!"

"Nothing's happening," said Lulu and Pippa impatiently.
Twinkle didn't give up. She flew as fast as she could over
Fairy Godmother's garden, wildly waving her wand and shouting,

"Think PINK!
Think PINK!
Quick, turn everything
PINKETY PINK!"

Fairy Godmother's roses shook and swayed.

Then they rocked and they rolled . . .

Poof! Every single rose turned pink as a flamingo! And that's not all . . .
Fairy Godmother's hedges turned pink, her grass turned pink,
and even her canary turned pink!

"Wowee!"
Lulu exclaimed.

"Super-duper!"
Pippa laughed.

"Trolls and toadstools!" Twinkle cried.
"What will Fairy Godmother say?"

Twinkle spun around in the sky, crazily waving her wand and shouting,

"Go away pink,
fly to the moon~
don't come back
anytime soon!"

But the harder she tried, the pinker everything in the garden became.
It was a candy floss and bubblegum pink fantasy land!

"Glittering gumdrops!" cried Twinkle,
and she flew off to see Fairy Godmother.

"Goodness me, Twinkle," said Fairy Godmother in surprise. "I've been working for weeks coloring the roses for my party."

Twinkle's wings drooped and turned from rosy pink to blue. "I was trying out a fancy new spell," she explained.

"You're a powerful little fairy," said Fairy Godmother, "and it's good to try out new things. Now show me your pink wish, please."

Twinkle and Fairy Godmother flew off together to see the garden. And when Fairy Godmother saw all the pink, she stopped and laughed out loud.

"Of course I love every color, but my favorite is pink," she said.
"Is it yours, too?"
Twinkle nodded.

"We'll keep those perfectly pink roses for the garden party tomorrow," announced Fairy Godmother. "They go nicely with all the latest Fairyland fashions."

The next day Twinkle and her fairy friends dressed
up in their most sparkly outfits and went to Fairy
Godmother's Perfectly Pink Party.

They had a wonderful time eating fairy cakes,
singing fairy songs, and dancing the fairy fandango.

Twinkle's heart was glowing with happiness,

and that's when something

fairytastic happened . . .

. . . her little wings began to glow and sparkle,
and her fairy power grew and grew!
Twinkle smiled and made a wish . . .

"Rainbow colors,
come back soon
under the sun
and under the moon!"

Then Twinkle gently waved
her wand and poof!

All the roses turned back to
their rainbow colors again.
"Hurray for Twinkle power!"
everyone cried.

FEB 2020
(2014)

Tabitha

Lulu

Pippa

Petal

Twinkle

Buttercup

Izzybell